A GUIDE TO OVERSTANDING LOVE

THE

STAY WOKE

SERIES

WHAT IS LOVE ?

NATHANIEL J. ALI

THE
STAY WOKE
SERIES

What is Love?

By: Nathaniel J. Ali

Copyright

Table of Contents

Chapter 1 WHO AM I?
Do you see the problem?
....
............................14

Chapter 2 PURPOSE
....
............................33

Chapter 3 WOMAN & MAN
....
............................44

Chapter 4 DEATH & GOD
....
............................55

Chapter 5 FINDING LOVE
....
............................68

Chapter 6 WORDS OF ADVICE

....
............................82

Chapter 7 NOTES

....
............................105

Dedication

I dedicate this book to The Most High God, Jah who has given me the strength to endure and overcome everything that I have been through and will encounter in the future. I thank you for blessing me with vision and purpose. I see now that I needed to stay awake when everyone else was sleeping in order to evolve, transition, and work when no one was looking.

I dedicate this book to my Mother and sister, who have seen me evolve and fall a plethora of times. I thank you for your patience and for teaching me. I thank you for letting me Rise. More importantly, thank you for not giving up on me.

I dedicate this book to my Father. We have not always seen eye to eye but, I have learned that iron sharpens iron and often times a terrible battle spares a deadly war.

I dedicate this book to my future Queen. Knowing that you exist, knowing that you possess a type of love that I have never experienced, knowing that I will be able to walk by your side and lead you to better, and that I will meet you has taught me how to be more optimistic and find self love. The thought of you, has helped me find myself. I greatly appreciate you and I am extremely grateful to The Most High that I will have the pleasure of meeting you, protecting you, loving you, aiding you, and supporting you. Knowing that you exist has led to my inner awakening, Chapter 5 is dedicated to you. You have changed my heart in a way that I never knew was possible. You are the essence of life itself and this beast would be nothing without the beauty that is within you.

I dedicate this book to every woman that I have met and those that I have hurt. I thank you for entering my life while I was hurting and trying to understand love. You came into my life for a reason and I am grateful for the lessons. It was never my intention to hurt you and I hope you can forgive my mistakes and untimely misfortune.

OVERSTANDING

The definition of Overstanding is not one that is commonly understood.

Overstanding is the ability to grasp the root and the inner meaning of a concept, phrase, experience, or lesson. Once the root and the inner meaning of something has been internalized and applied to an individual's life, that individual is then said to have reached a higher level of being and thinking.

I would like to thank the beautiful model Jasmine Holeman, my good friend and Creative Director Raven Nicole Giggs, Deborah May, Photographer Vernon Samuel, and BJ Watson.

Blessings,

I have learned that we as a people enslave ourselves mentally. We discount our love for someone else's satisfaction. Majority of the time we are blinded by fear and a lack of understanding. We try to control things but, still protest that we are walking by faith. How can we walk by faith and not by sight, if we choose to only believe what we see? I am guilty of leaning to my own understanding. However, the goal is to inner-stand and over-stand. I accept every walk of life, person, and religion. Although I do not believe in religion, my choice to regulate myself according to THE MOST HIGH and his/her mandate is my perspective. I welcome you to my thoughts and a part of my spirit, in hopes that we can both mutually benefit from this experience. I realize that my truth may not be someone else's truth.

Once awakening to a higher state of consciousness I decided to overstand the very essence of life and the true meaning of the pursuit of happiness. This is spiritual, not worldly. We are not of the world, we are of spirit. My fear is a production of trauma and pain that has consumed my life. Both subconsciously and consciously. Without knowing it, I was never really in pain but, instead I continued to manifest the same experiences over and over again. My inability to heal is what caused me to experience pain. I chose to not acknowledge the lessons that I encountered and experienced. I willingly chose to ignore what THE MOST HIGH revealed to me. This led to my downfall and countless failures. Why? I subconsciously acted and lived through pain and not purpose. I functioned through fear and not faith. I resided in ego and walked with pride.

This is a lesson that I cannot deny or choose to not see. The Most High has snatched me from the very pit of my lower self by forcing the higher version of thyself to take over. As a person, you have no choice but to ascend. Meaning, you have no choice but to receive THE VERY BEST that is destined for you. Keep in mind that we serve a just creator, who not only wants the best for us but, loves us enough to grant us free will. Sadly, we as a people abuse that free will and that is why we do NOT receive THE VERY BEST that is destined for us. There's no more unbalance. There are no more questions. I know my path. I know my way. It does not matter what my Mother or Father says. It does not matter what religion says. It does not matter what the institutions that have been created by men have to say. It does not matter what anyone says. I cannot live for them. I must live for me and walk as a sacrificial lamb for THE MOST HIGH.

I choose to stand as the embodiment of love. The sacrificial lamb, I am. That is a spirit that we must all adapt to. Have I always been that way? No. This life is a journey, it is a process and no man nor woman is perfect. We all struggle with something and must overcome an inner battle within. I have found myself. Some people believe that you cannot transform overnight. I disagree. I do not believe in the concept of time because time is an illusion. It is infinite. Life is unlimited, the only thing that ages or is categorized by time is that which depends on the elements and certain variables. That is the physical. Our vessel. Your body is just a vehicle transporting a soul, that is what ages. However, you are not a body, you are a spirit therefore the fountain of youth is within you.

What you choose to believe that which is just, beneficial to you and the world, that which betters life, that which is of THE MOST HIGH and not of ego or ignorance. What you choose to believe internally, will manifest from the inside out. This determines how you will live. This determines how your vessel will function. However, there are certain principles and keys to this philosophy that I have adapted. This perspective will be for another book. Time was created by man. Man invented the concept of time. I choose to operate on the time of The Most High and for that reason alone, time does not exist. There is no such thing as day and night. There is only life. There is only light. Yes, darkness does exist. However, light can live within darkness but, darkness cannot live within light. Time is linear and because of that it is abundant. The amount of time that it has taken you to get to know someone, does not determine how much or how little you love them or how much they may love you.

What is love? Do we love? Or, do we exist because of love? Or, does love exist because of us? I believe that is up for interpretation. As I reflect upon my past relationships and situationships, I realize my role and the part that I played in every scenario. My pain and my lack of self awareness produced narcissistic tendencies that I did not realize I brought into my relationships. I functioned through ego and pride, not love. However, if the only form of love that you have seen is that which is shown through ego and pride, what do you do? Simple. You acknowledge that you have not seen nor experienced love. You may have experienced a form of love but, it was not healthy love.

I sit in shame when reflecting but, I realize that it was not about "What did I go through to make me that way?" It was simply a question of, how do I change? How do I deprogram? How do I reprogram? How do I learn the true meaning of unconditional love? How do I unlearn? How do I develop better interpersonal skills? The answer is simple. It is a matter of first acknowledging and then the process begins. Once you become aware of your flaws, you begin to work on them without knowing it. I am thankful for the lessons because they have built me and are leading me to the blessings that are meant for me. They have led me to my blessing(s), which are gratitude, faith, forgiveness, peace, and more. Appreciation for what is and what was. More importantly an appreciation for what will be.

Before you begin to read this book, I pray that you read it with an open mind. I pray that it becomes cleansing fruit for your body so that you may multiply and move accordingly. As a man, I pray that the men and the young men that read this book will learn from the mistakes that I share within these pages and realize that love itself starts from within. As a son and a brother, I pray that the women and the young women that read this book will see these words and allow it to become sweet honey and natural milk, which will nourish every broken bone and organ in your body, giving you everlasting life and a foundation for increase.

The Most High spoke to me one day while I was sitting in class listening to a lecture on Audre Lorde. It was a quick download and expansion of my perspective, which brought a feeling of peace to my mind, body, and spirit. I immediately turned to a blank page in my notebook and wrote these words:

"Do not be afraid of those who speak ill of you. The truth is only evident within the spirit of those who do not follow. Your truth may not be their truth. Your truth is only meant for those who will lead and not follow. You must adapt to this perspective. I think, therefore I am. I feel, therefore I become. I see what is not seen, therefore I believe. Walk by faith and not by sight. Stay true to me and you will see, truly see."

Regards,

Nathaniel J. Ali

CHAPTER 1
WHO AM I?

Do you see the problem?   .

Often times, we later learn that our gift is something that we discovered during our childhood, without knowing that it was a gift. My love for literature began in the third or fourth grade with a thanks to my beautiful Mother and J.K. Rowling. As a child who grew up being teased and isolated, I did my best to see the good in everyone that I encountered, except myself. In 2011 I entered my first year of college at North Carolina Central University (NCCU) and I fell in attraction time and time again. I thought that the woman that I was "in love with" was the one. I failed to realize that my love was merely infatuation, deep appreciation, codependency, and a lack of self awareness which allowed me to attach myself to someone because of an insecurity and a false sense of self. This is what love was for me as a Freshman in college. I have had a recurring problem of seeing the gold in every woman I encounter on a certain level.

Unfortunately, I failed to see the gold in myself. Life is about evolving, maturing, and transitioning. However, I have come to realize that if you are not holistically mature on a certain level or surface, you will not be blessed with your next opportunity.

At the age of 25, I can humbly say that I do not have to struggle as I did in the past. Is my bank account where I would like for it to be? No. But, I have come so far spiritually, mentally, emotionally, and physically that I am grateful for who I have become. To me, that is wealth. That is stability. Not money. Money, just like time is a manmade concept. Why should something that is not of the spirit determine how I govern myself? I wrote this book with the intentions of being a helpful voice so that the stereotypical man will realize that it is okay to acknowledge and tend to your own emotions. It's okay to transition. It's okay to grow. Sometimes, I find that nursing your mental will lead to healthy emotions. You have to become better equipped spiritually. What you lack and what has not been instilled in you, must instill within yourself. You have to become a warrior and be willing to battle within yourself in order to advance to your next stage in life.

So, the question is "Who Am I?" Honestly, the normal answer would be to give you my name, a brief summarization of my life, maybe toss in a quote that describes myself, a subliminal prayer, and a background story of my parent's relationship. Instead, I will simply focus on dealing with the issue at hand, which is me. I am the issue. I am the subject. Greater is he that is in us and the sooner that you realize that, everything that I tell you in this book will begin to make sense.

With this particular book, the history of relationships and their impact on me personally, is not important. It is my reaction to these experiences that needs to be the focus. In each chapter I will establish a guide pertaining to each chapter and topic. However, I will not give you everything you need to know within these pages, you'll have to keep purchasing the books that will follow this one. Why? Because, in my generation we have become lost. We have become lost in this world and within ourselves. We have lost sight of who created us. Thus, we instead worship false images, idols, electronics, people, and materialistic objects. We rather party than to save a life. We rather record a traumatic event than to pray or help. We rather get drunk, high, and have meaningless sex with people than to walk in our purpose. We demoralize our own beliefs and values because we allow for man-made concepts and structures to govern us. We have began to do the very thing that The Most High instructed us not to do.

Which is what exactly?

A Pastor would tell you, that the answer would be to turn to your bible and then proceed by giving a scripture to read. However, I am not a Pastor. The Most High, your creator, whomever you believe that to be wants you to worship "Him/ Her." You are to worship the entity/spirit that created all things, including you. The Universe. We, as the lost generation have begun to worship objects and thus have been given the name "millennials."

As I begin to write this book, I decided to look at old poetry that I have written and coincidentally enough, I found the first one that I have ever written for a woman, which was written in 2011.

Loving Disability

By:

Nathaniel J. Ali

Beauty is in the eye of the beholder

Even if I was blind I could still see you

If the world was suddenly covered in darkness

Your phlegmatic skin tone and smile let alone your

presence

Would brighten my day, let alone my world.

Joy and happiness versus you would hold no weight

Like a tumor on one's heart

I have to get you off of me.

Charismatic smile and personality

So rare that it could make Aphrodite herself

The goddess of love turn her head in shame

Compassion and perseverance is your DNA

Let alone your genetic physical make-up.

So… is to stare to annoy?

Or to observe and read so that in the future

You could hope to take care of the studied object

Love it as if it were gold itself

You are gold.

Do you see the problem?

I will humbly say that this is a well crafted poem that simply shows how a young man (me) feels for the woman at the point in time it was written. *Do you see the problem?* If you read the poem carefully you will see the lack of discipline and love for one's self. Also, you will notice that at the very end of the poem, I state "Or to observe and read so that in the future… You could hope to take care of the studied object… Love it as if it were gold itself… You are gold."

We will now take each line and analyze it. One thing that I have learned about myself and my generation is that we lean too far one way, we have a hard time finding balance. We have a hard time balancing head and heart. Thus, we confuse infatuation and lust with love. We either lean too far into the past and lose focus or we lean too far into the future and lose focus.

The first line that I recited says, "Or to observe and read so that in the future…" First, men… please do not make the mistake of trying to read a woman because you will lose every time. You cannot read a woman, they can read you. You must use the spirit of discernment when dealing with a woman. That way of being I have adapted to but, I cannot teach you that within these pages. You would have to schedule a Life and Spiritual Coaching session with me via email. You can only guess and assume. In addition,

I would like to add that you should never assume in regards to women. Just wait. *Do you see the problem?*

I made the mistake of wanting to be with a woman so bad that I wanted to read her and study her as if she was a course taught in school. Research shows that men within this society are barely graduating as is, African-American men especially. So, why would I willingly choose to study a living being, knowing that I have not adopted study habits that can lead me to an "A" in my classes? I'll let you sit on that and answer that for yourself. I was thinking too far ahead into the future, not focusing enough in the present moment. I didn't focus enough on the present to receive the blessing. *Do you see the problem?*

The second line states, "You could hope to take care of the studied object..." Once again, I will say that you cannot assume anything pertaining to women. You either know or you don't. *Do you see the problem?* I do. The problem with this line is "the studied object." Without knowing it, I showed my lack of maturity by writing this poem and those three words added an exclamation. You can never treat a woman like an object or a foreign creature in its natural habitat. I will make this statement now. In my opinion, you cannot find anything more exotic or foreign than the African woman or the woman of the African Diaspora. Unfortunately, I'm sharing a poem that was written when I was eighteen years of age. This is due to the poorly constructed and evolved mindset and traditions of European society and the desired image of "Utopia," the "American dream."

What is America? What is American? Colonization and imperialism. Many young men of the African Diaspora grow up with this mindset because of the illusion of the "American Dream." Audre Lorde once said, "The white fathers told us: I think, therefore I am. The Black mother within each of us - the poet - whispers in our dreams: I feel, therefore I can be free." Nevertheless, institutionalization leads to dehumanization.

As a young man in this "halfway" house called a society, you are taught that YOU, the MAN are the hunter. The woman, is the prey. We are sadly mistaken and must rid ourselves of this false teaching. There is no hunter or prey when mentioning affairs of the spirit and more importantly, women. Now, there may be a subconsciously narcissistic man reading this book and saying, that I must be sexually deprived or lacking thereof in some department pertaining to my physicality. You are sadly mistaken my friend. The only thing deprived in this situation is your brain and the lack of oxygen that it is getting due to your inability to acknowledge or be content with the presentation of another perspective, that may be different from yours.

Man: That's BLASPHEMY!

Me: How so?

Man: I have a career, I have a family, I have more than one degree, and I'm brilliant!

Me: My brother, you are poorly mistaken and I advise you to continue reading this book.

Reggae artist and a well known brother of the Rastafari community Tony Rebel once said, "What is wrong with the yutes of today? Is the BABYLON system leading them astray." We live in a society that teaches you to be the hunter when pursuing a relationship, not the King that your Queen needs. We live in a society that teaches you to twerk rather than pray. Work a 9-5, rather than meditate and find peace. We live in a society that isn't even aware that many forms of dancing, such as "twerking" originated in Africa. Though it may not look the same.

May I also add that it is and was not trashy looking as it is in this society. We live in a society that teaches you that eating meat and drinking milk from an animal is beneficial to your body. They won't teach you that the life expectancy rate in America is less than 78 years of age (as of 2015), while countries such as Japan exceeds above 83.84 (as of 2015). This is not hidden information and easily be found on google. We live in a society that rather build statues in remembrance of certain members of the KKK, rather than the Africans who were forced to be slaves and build this country with their bare hands.

Do you see the problem?

The third and fourth line in the poem states, "Love it as if it were gold itself... You are gold." This is probably the only thing in the poem that makes sense. To love a woman as if she was gold itself, you are gold. Some men and women probably cannot begin to fathom what that feels like. Most men in this society and generation rather invest in gold, than to invest in their woman. Forgetting that their woman is more valuable than gold. Most women rather chase the gold, than to become the gold. This mentality is what classifies us as "The Lost Generation."

The Most High will only allow for you to get but so far, if something in your character does not meet his approval. Why? Because he doesn't want your gift that can build you, to kill you before you have a chance to use it for his glory. Majority of us cannot receive our blessing because we are busy living for the approval of a thousand, when we should only live for the approval of one. We turn down one person who wants to love us, for the company of a few who only wish to turn up with us and do not add to our spirit. They add to our insecurities and the illusion that we have created for ourselves. They do not add to our purpose. They add to our pain and we embrace it.

My Mother once told me, "You're tapping into your gift and calling at such a mighty force." But, I thought to myself when she said that and I realized that I was unstable because I was not able to handle the force that came with the realization of who I am as a man. I acknowledged that their was a calling on my life but, because I chose to walk by sight and not faith, I led myself blindly to experiences that I could have avoided. But, because my path was already prewritten and my footsteps have been ordained, what I have been through worked for me and not against me. What people thought would break me, only built me!

As I'm writing this book, I feel happy enough with myself to say that I accept whatever responsibility comes with the calling on my life and whatever The Most High chooses to place on my shoulders I will happily do. At your service! So, "Who Am I?" I am a man who continues to find himself everyday. I am a man who continues to ask for forgiveness even when I haven't done anything wrong, in my eyes. I realize my part in situations. I'm not perfect. I am flawed beyond measure. However, everyday I am learning how to fight addictions because, I know that I can't do it alone. I am learning what it means to be a King and still acknowledge the man that I use to be. I am learning what it means to be wise. I am learning what it means to be humble. I am learning how to continuously tap into the God within. More importantly, I am learning what it means to be human and dehumanized.

We all make mistakes. It doesn't matter if you rank as a high office government official, a person who lacks common sense, or someone who is solely influenced by money. Lord forbid if you're all three but, I digress. We are all prone to make mistakes. It is our reaction that defines us. It is what we choose to do that determines our character. If you fall down seven times, all it takes is that one chance for you to get back up and start a new beginning. Understand, inner-stand, and overstand that all relationships will NOT start off perfectly. You and your partner may get into a fight and stop talking to each other for days, weeks, or maybe months. But, it's the recovery process and your reaction that determines the outcome, as well as your character. Your ability to recognize your inability to carry out certain things will say more about you than your first kiss. I do not know if this book will solve all of your problems but, I guarantee you that it will point you in the right direction.

If you are broken then I suggest that you ask the divine for healing. Talk to your higher self and I do not mean the version of you that is not sober. I suggest that you understand that you may have pushed someone away unintentionally but, it's okay. You're human, no one is perfect. Pray that the Lord heals the part of you that holds you as a prisoner to yourself. Forgive the people that have hurt you and done you wrong. Forgive your past. Embrace the present and walk forward into the future. Everyday when you wake up, pray and thank The Most High for all that you have. Every moment that you get a chance to, tell the Lord thank you. Before you go to sleep, pray. Look in the mirror and realize that you are not your past. You are your future and that is determined by how you choose to live in the present.

You are a gift from above. Make the effort to push forward and realize that nothing is your fault and you are everything that is love. You are strong. You are beautiful. You are intelligent. You are everything that you never knew you could be. Forgive the person that hurt you. Forgive the people that hurt you. You are no longer your situation. The past is the past and it is never coming back. But, blessings won't come into your life until you walk away from the past. Keep your head high and above everything else, guard your heart. But, do not lock it. Because in the midst of a chain heart will bring forth confusion and you will stray away from the key. Do not fear love. Do not turn away from it. Embrace it.

CHAPTER 2
PURPOSE

During the summer of 2016, I attended community college and my life was changed forever once entering the classroom of a Professor, who is a small woman that made a tremendous impact on my life, as well as my ability to articulate my story. Out of many assignments, one stands out to me the most and that is the same speech that I happened to give when I participated in a Ted Talk, on April 1st (you can find it on YouTube entitled "Vision and Purpose Nathaniel Peterkin"). The speech was about an Aesop Fable entitled "The Ant and the Chrysalis" and how it applied to my life. The Ant and the Chrysalis is about an Ant who was searching for food and happened to come across a Chrysalis that was near its time of change, attracting the attention of the Ant who realized that it was alive. The Ant pitied the Chrysalis and felt as if it was beneath him. Telling the Chrysalis that it had a sad fate, bragging about how it was able to run freely and was not imprisoned by a shell. The Chrysalis heard the Ant but, did not reply.

A few days passed and the Ant returned to where he first saw the Chrysalis but, he saw nothing. The Chrysalis appeared with wings as a beautiful butterfly and said to the Ant, "Behold in me your much-pitied friend, now I am free". The Butterfly told the Ant to continue to boast for there was no reason for him to listen. He rose in the air and flew out of sight from the Ant, never to return. From this small story and from my own philosophy I gathered that "Appearances are deceptive" and fate is never really understood. Appearances are defined as the way someone or something looks. Fate is defined as the development of events beyond a person's control. Often times, we may look at a person and think that because they look a certain way that they must choose this path or that path, without taking into consideration who the person is on the inside.

Confucius once said, "Everything has beauty but, not everyone sees it." What is beauty? Do you see it? It took me twenty five years to understand that there is beauty in life itself and that life itself is beautiful. Life is merely an imitation of art.

Most people would never know that I am the CEO and Founder of TRI FIT USA (specializes in holistic health by placing emphasis on personal training, life coaching, and spiritual teaching), NALI Non-Profit Corporation, and DÃN FASHION LLC (athletic apparel). I started my first company in January of 2016. I started this company because I strongly believe that holistic living is the key to higher living. My TEDx speech was based on a personal experience in which within four years I became a drug dealer who barely knew what he was doing and homeless, while sleeping in a car with a 4 week old puppy for a period of 8 months I gave too much of myself to the wrong people. Do you see the problem?

Many people cannot begin to fathom what it takes to reposition yourself and begin creating your own business while becoming the CEO, ascending, deprogramming, learning, healing, and being able to graduate with an Associate in Arts degree in the year 2017. Thankfully, I have positioned myself to receive a Bachelor's Degree with the anticipated graduation year of December 2019, learning a foreign language, and I even tried out for professional football, a week after being in a car accident and hitting my head on the windshield. I came, I saw, and I conquered my goal with a 4.58 in the 40 yard dash. Not only does it take grace but, it takes grit. I learned that from Sarah Jakes Roberts.

The journey was and is still painful. I am still having to de-institutionalize myself. My parents probably aren't aware that when I moved back home with them, I had to teach myself how to use a debit card all over again and a phone. I was so use to using the bathroom in the woods and the bushes that a toilet often times felt foreign to me. It has taken me until now (2018), to get comfortable sleeping in a bed. I was so use to sleeping in a car in a upright position that I often times slept on the floor back home because the bed wasn't as comfortable. One thing that I learned from this is that, a person does not go higher than their environment. Throughout my period of homelessness I was looked down on, laughed at, misunderstood, used, and taken for granted time and time again. So, what is a man to do? Simple. Change his environment.

Throughout my whole life it seemed as if I was headed in the right direction but, I never really understood that along the way I was doing anything and everything to make my family happy but, I never did what made me happy. It appeared to everyone that I was happy and content with my life but, having battled with depression and suicide since the age of 8 or 9, not telling anyone because I didn't think anyone cared. I realized that I never did anything to make myself happy. That became my life, making others happy. That is what I begin to base my purpose and functioning off of, making others happy. Which is not living. That very existence is the closest thing to death that you can feel. Because you're not living within yourself or adding to your spirit. You're living without and adding to the egos of others at the expense of your spirit.

I never understood what actual happiness was nor did I know how it felt. I started participating in sports and clubs when I was younger because everyone around me told me that I would be good at it. I started playing basketball in the fourth grade and kept playing through high school. I was invited to basketball camps, combines, and reached out to by lower Division schools. Everyone pushed me since a young age. I remember certain family members coming to my games, congratulating me on my performance but, I rarely remember someone asking me how I was doing or how I felt.

My parents instilled in me the ability to push forward. Strength is my greatest attribute, it runs through my veins, it's in my genetic makeup, it shows in my appearance but, I didn't know how to be strong for myself until I was all by myself. Sadly, I find that being the case today. Alone physically. Sometimes you must be isolated so that you can realize that you're never alone spiritually. I do my best to elaborate on that because the divine is always with us. The universe is always with us. Entering my first year of college wasn't a very outgoing experience for me. But, because of my Speech and Debate background I knew how to engage in conversation with people, especially women. However, I lacked experience in socializing and everyday life. In middle school and high school I rarely went out in public, I never dated and never had a girlfriend. I never had a conversation with anyone about relationships or women. I rarely had anyone talk to me about the actual college experience. Because I was so studious and athletic, everyone assumed that I was ready for the outside world but, I was never equipped with the essentials only the hardware. I was the chosen one and the forgotten one.

As I look back on my life, I realize that all of the people that treated me badly and judged me were just a test. Everyone around me was the Ant, they told me how pitiful I was, they bragged about their circumstances, laughed at me, used me, abused me, and misunderstood my situation. I was criticized based on my circumstance. Because I was homeless people believed that I wasn't educated and less than a person. I was stuck in my Chrysalis for more than two years but, I didn't spread my wings and turn into a Butterfly until the Ants left and I was able to break free of my situation and embrace my isolation.

Our purpose in life is to evolve. We are meant to identify our gift which will aid us in exercising our vision.

Your gift is your vehicle which will carry you and transport you to your vision. You must treat your gift like an actual vehicle. You must provide it with the right type of fuel, take care of it, do not allow for anyone to damage it or taint it, or abuse your gift. I have learned that you must trust your instincts as well as your purpose. Those two things combined will bring you everlasting overflow of abundance for you and your family. My purpose in life is to help mankind and it took me till recently to understand exactly how to do that. In order to change the world we must change ourselves but, before we can help the world, we must first help ourselves.

Truthfully, I'm excited. My strength resides inside of me and not anyone else. I found beauty in life itself and once I became aware and content, I regained my strength. I do not require validation, only love and the fact that it is 12:12 AM on New Years Day 1/1/2018 and I'm finishing this book (Note: It is 9:12 AM on 10/2/2018 and I am adding little things to these pages that I have learned, which I feel will benefit both you and I) shows me that I am on the right path. I urge whomever is reading this book to identify your gift and find your vision. Pray on it. Meditate on it. Through that you will find your purpose in life. You will stop existing and understand what it means to truly live. The goal however, is to inner-stand and transition to overstanding your destiny. This will come over time.

CHAPTER 3
WOMAN & MAN

I have a lot of respect for women, especially African women and those of the African Diaspora. I strongly believe that my sisters, these Queens are the most powerful beings that have ever walked this earth. To think that I as a man was birthed and taught by a woman, I was raised by a woman, nurtured by a woman, and fought for by a woman. That amazes me. Queen. Thank you Momma. I however realize that as a man I am still not completely 100% able to ascend into a higher version of myself without a woman by my side. It is my responsibility to walk my path alone but, be open to someone who is conducive and healthy enough to walk with me and support me.

I lay awake at night and sometimes I never sleep because I wonder if there is someone in this world for me, someone who compliments me, accepts me, and will walk beside me. You may see a woman in a picture with me in this book however, she is a model and a friend of mine. I made a post on Instagram one day and the picture said, "I'm 24 years of age and I have never held hands with a woman in public." I've never experienced PDA. That all changed a year later and only lasted for three weeks. Although the ending was painful, I'm grateful that The Most High granted me that small opportunity. Quite frankly, I use to be afraid of rejection. I was afraid of rejection because I was insecure and constant rejection led to my insecurities. I've been rejected within every relationship and situationship. Yes. I do play a part in it but, what I'm simply trying to say in the oddest and most painful way is that deep down I respect women. They are the world's best teacher.

It may not sound like it but, as a man who has been hurt countless times by women, I honestly have respect for them. Why? Because no other living being has the power to uplift a man to the highest version of himself and also possess enough power to snatch the world from under his feet. In my opinion, the closest thing to God that any man will ever see is a woman. In my eyes, mind, body, and spirit the closest thing to God for me is, the African woman. Including the woman of the African Diaspora. Who else can give birth to a civilization, endure slavery, be the right hand to a man, the backbone, endure heartbreak, separation, inequality, and raise a King? As a man, we often make the mistake and assume that women need us. THEY DO NOT. Women do NOT need a man. A man needs a woman. A woman only wants a man that can aid and compliment her.

Why? Women are able to harness their feminine energy, which is where creation and life come from, the feminine energy. At the same time, a woman is able to tap into her masculine side as well, masculine energy. This is where boundaries and dominion come from. They are strong enough to do both and learn how to do so, quicker than men but also more efficiently. Men on the other hand, are a mess. We are so masculine, thanks to society, that when we begin to subconsciously tap into our feminine energy we aren't aware of it. We have been told to ignore it, to ignore certain feelings. However, in order for anyone to grow they must tap into both energies.

Majority of the time, when a man taps into his feminine side and has never experienced it, he will act irrational and start to seem crazy because he doesn't know what it is that he's feeling. He doesn't know how to articulate his new found emotions. He can't locate it. He can't understand why he is crying at certain times when he's thinking about a woman he's in love with or a death in his family. Men have been programmed to ignore their emotions thus, making them a walking coke bottle that is constantly being shaken and not stirred. He is dangerous to no one but, himself. However, his current partner will feel the effects from this.

When this happens, if the man's partner is strong enough to approach the man and ask what's going on or explain to them that their behavior is and has been irrational, a better and more fruitful relationship can stem from this.

Often times, as men we are use to being in control but, when things are out of our control we begin to act outside of our character. However, what I've learned is that how you act during times when nothing is in your control and the level of patience equipped with it, determines how much of a King you are. A man is a human, so naturally he will act out because he is still in touch with his lowest self and his inner child. But, a King is closer to God and is able to acknowledge his inner child.

A King is able to learn patience and may not be perfect at it but, he can practice it and acknowledge his inner child. Are you as close to God as you think?

I will be perfectly honest and say that a man can only become a King once touched in a certain way by a Queen. Whether that be good or indifferent. Bad does not exist, there is only indifferent. The concept of "bad" is a perspective. If the right woman can embrace that man and talk through the problems, she will be blessed beyond measure, if that man is a God fearing man. However, many women want a man that is already made. A lot of women want a man that already has a six figure income, an updated car, a house, no children, no insecurities, a career, amazing sex game, and is already self made. NEWS FLASH!! No man is ever that self made. I do not care how well a man seems to be put together, he will never be fully equipped with everything that you want.

If you are a woman in your mid-twenties and you meet a man who has a degree, is working towards another degree, has a nice car, self employed, articulate, moderately comprehensive in a foreign language, has a place of residence, is a man of God, likes to workout, is exercising his gift, and is willing to put forth effort with you. Is that not good enough? For some women, the answer would be yes. But, what if that man had a painful past? Would you want him then? Would you want him, even if he was bettering himself and working on healing? Simple, no. Why? Because of the "baggage." Unfortunately, I am that man, at least I use to be. Most women want a man who is already getting the ball rolling. They don't want a man with all of that baggage.

Note: I have taken the liberty of periodically going back to read through this book before making it available to public and I would like to say that a some words within this book show brokenness. However, I want you to see growth in this book so, I have decided to leave certain things in it. Dying alone is not an option. We were not made to die alone. A person chooses to die alone. Those women in my past only hurt me because I ALLOWED FOR THEM TO DO SO. It doesn't matter what they have done to me or what they have said to me. It doesn't matter if they asked for space and dumped me via text. What I have learned (as of 3/18/18) is that you control the power over your life and by allowing for someone to bring you out of your character, you give them that power over you. YOU MUST TAKE YOUR POWER BACK!

PTDD

I developed this term and diagnoses myself.

We have all heard of PTSD, Post Traumatic Stress Disorder which is characterized by a person who has difficulty functioning throughout everyday life due to a horrible situation that they witnessed or experienced. According to www.ptsd.ne.gov/ a percentage of roughly 7.8 people will experience PTSD in their life. Women being 10.4% and men being 5%. The average diagnosis is given to people between the ages of 18 to their early 50s. This is true, this is real. This is an issue. But, what if the same could be applied to dating and the experiences that we get from them?

My single life has been tougher than most people can imagine. I've been in one or two relationships (give or take) and some situationships but, for some reason PDA has always lacked. In the past I use to wonder why but, after a while I stopped asking. The first step in moving forward to becoming a better person is acknowledging your problems and flaws. I have a cold side to me in addition to an insecure side which comes from my past experiences. A lot of men and women wonder at times, why there partner doesn't do or say certain things in private or public. Often times, the answer is simple.

"Post Traumatic Dating Disorder (PTDD)" which is a term I would like to define. PTDD is a lightly used term that is used to highlight key areas of a persons dating life that shows as to why that person has a hard time thriving in their current partnership. My advice to anyone dealing with a partner with PTDD is to TALK to them, talk it out, and work it out. PTDD is not permanent. When "I" is replaced with "we" even illness becomes wellness.

CHAPTER 4
GOD & Death

As I'm writing this book the old me is dying and the
new me is coming into the now and the light. My Mother

always told me that death and life are in the power of the tongue and I never believed her until I started writing this book. *We must become reborn spiritually. Secondly, we must become reborn mentally. Thirdly, we must become reborn emotionally. I call it the holy trinity of self evolution.* The ability for a person to be rebirthed into a new creation by going deep within one's self and acknowledging every shortcoming, flaw, negative behavior, and poorly constructed way of thinking. Look within. Introspection.

We must experience death on some type of level and in some degree in order to know what it truly means to live. Death isn't scary. Dying isn't scary. However, I never believed that death itself was scary, it's only how we die or how we choose to let ourselves die that is scary.

Below, I have provided space for you to write. The instructions are simple. *I want you to list 5-10 things about yourself that you want to leave your spirit right now.* I want you to write them in **ALL CAPS** and then *explain why.* This is a release exercise and a way for you to rid yourself of what is no longer working for you.

1) _____

_____

_____

_____

_____

2) _____

_____

_____

_____

_____

3) _____

_____

_____

_____

_____

4) _____

_____

_____

_____

_____

5) _____

_____

_____

_____

_____

6) _____

_____

_____

7) _____

8) _____

9) _____

10) _____

_____

_____

_____

_____

After you have written what you would like to rid yourself of, I want you to say this affirmation and repeat these words aloud:

"MOST HIGH, I ask for the release of my own imprisonment. I ask that you allow what is not helping me to grow to leave me, starting now! From this day forward I no longer want to walk in darkness. From this day forward I no longer want to walk with death. I have seen the error of my ways and I am ready to change. I am ready to be better. I am ready for preparation. I am ready for

rejuvenation. I am ready to start and endure the race that you have given me. I know that the race is not given to the swift but, to those who can endure. I have been selfishness. I ask for forgiveness. I have been disobedient and I did not see what you had created for me this entire time. Thank you."

Now, let's get to the best part about this book "God." Who needs no introduction. The ALPHA and the OMEGA. THE BEGINNING and THE END! The divine that has been given meaning names but, yet we all serve the same creator. The Most High has blessed me beyond measure and I am grateful for who I have become. I cannot thank him/ her enough and no action that I do can pay back or show him/ her how much grateful I am. I have my down days but, the thing is that there are less of them and they don't last as long as they use to. Jah has given me strength from a place within that I never knew existed until I had no choice but, to stand on it.

So, I thank you! I wrote this part of the book with a smile on my face because it brought me joy to know that I have been chosen to carry out this assignment. This particular mission was and has been designed for me and me only. No one can carry out or execute this mission the way that I do and will. That is my new mindset and that is me walking by faith and not by sight.

You have chosen me to fight through all of these hardships. You knew that I possessed something that others didn't. You knew that if anyone else were to be given what you put in front of me, they would have not overcome the those trials and tribulations the way that I have. Not saying that they wouldn't have made. I am simply saying that our journey through and after the storm would have been different because we are very different. I say that as humbly as possible.

I love your grace because it gave me grit. My belly is full but, I'm yearning for more. No more hardships such as those in the past because they were used to build me, not break me but, more opportunity to bring glory to your name. I'm yearning for a chance to put a smile on your face. I'm yearning for the opportunity that you have birthed me for. I am here MOST HIGH and I am ready! I am David and ready to face Goliath. I have made it out of the Lion's Den and will become one of the Kings to sit at your feet as Daniel did.

You have prepared me to be a King. I gladly welcome every blessing and anything that you send my way. But, if I am not ready... I ask that you prepare me and guide me into becoming a rock and steadfast into the King that you have called me to be. The Most High is amazing, do you believe it? I know sometimes, it's hard to imagine that if someone or something loves us they will put us through hardships. What if I told you that The Most High has been testing you? What if I told you that The Most High has been preparing you like a signature dish? He is adding all of the ingredients and is now seasoning you and getting you right for harvest. You are being seasoned. YOU. ARE. BEING. SEASONED!!!!

There is no hate involved, there is no malice. There is only love. God wants to give you abundance and riches that only your spirit can enjoy, not the things of this world. Yes, we can encounter these things but, do not love them. They may be beautiful to the eye but, are not rich to the soul. These enchantments are not for you. They may have a certain price but, what Jah has to offer is priceless, timeless, and unlimited. Everlasting life. I am not a Pastor, I am not a Preacher, I am not a Minister, nor an evangelist. I am not religious, nor a religious leader. I am a spiritual being and claim no religion but, I do acknowledge that The

Most High God, Jah exist. As a soldier of the The Most High who has found a philosophy and a way of life that works, specifically for me. I am pleased to say that. I do not require, nor am I looking for a title in order to deliver a message. However, if someone wishes to give me one, that is a different story. I am merely a man.

In this part of the book, I ask that you become real with yourself. I ask that before turning to the next page, you humble yourself. I need you to pay attention to my words carefully.

Who do you think created the skies and the ocean? Who do you think created the lands and the animals that walk on it? It was not man, I assure you. Babylon honestly fools people by giving things incorrect dates and by tearing down what Jah has built and made. Man destroys and ruins. Jah is a loving God and the only one that is allowed to cast judgment on your soul or anyone for that matter. Man cannot condemn your spirit. I strongly believe that there is no right or wrong religion but, the belief in a higher power and the concept of who Immanuel was and is, is imperative. There is no right or wrong religion, there is only one way of loving. There are different perspectives but, we must learn to coexist. There is only one way of living.

Unfortunately, I can't wait but you understand. If you turn to 2 Corinthians 5:17 in your bible it says, "Anyone who is joined to Christ is a new being; the old is gone, the new has come." If you go to Romans 10:9-10, "If you confess that Immanuel is your Lord and believe that The Most High raised him from death, you will be saved. For it is by our faith that we are put right with God, it is by our confession that we are saved." I would like to add that the biggest mistake that we as humans have made is reading the bible and taking the words such as "raised from death" literally. Instead think of it metaphorically. Being raised from the dead could mean many things but, I strongly believe that when The Most High raised him from death, he was raised to a higher state of consciousness. He ascended. Therefore, he was elevated as a spiritual being and as a man. That is my perspective.

You must develop your own perspective that is conducive to your spirit and does not bring harm or infringe upon others. Learn the truth for yourself and remember that your truth may not be the truth for everyone else. I learned that from my good friend *Zeus*, who I've known since 2012.

CHAPTER 5
FINDING LOVE

If you read the dedication page of this book, then you will see that I dedicated this chapter to someone special. I am still single. Long story short, I wrote a letter to my future wife and Queen, which you will see below. I'm a Romantic and a Sapiosexual to the core and ever since I was little I have dreamt of being with a woman that I can call my best friend.

Dear Queen,

I am sorry that it has taken me so long to find you. In the past, I have chosen to focus on an outcome, rather than the issue. I've had to learn how to balance head and heart. More importantly I needed to find myself. I lost sight about what being God fearing truly is, it's a believer. A person who chooses to walk by faith, as are you. I'm ashamed of myself. I've only known how to receive one type of love and I never knew that another existed. Until the very thought of you saved me countless and countless times again. Dreaming about my children and their children.

I know that meeting you will aid me into becoming a better man and push me further to strengthen my walk with God. I know that you're a special woman. I look forward to sharing little dances with you, massaging you, comforting you, having conversations, and moments of transparency. I want to hold you and get lost in your vibration. I want to laugh with you. I want realness. I want to be open to showing you the real me, rather than trying to impress you and force it. I am a man who tends to suffer from pride and I don't ask for help. I probably will never ask for help majority of the time but, I ask that you be patient with me.

I realize that I can't keep going forward alone in this world. I've been stretched. I want to show you that I'm not the average man. I want to show you that I have dreams, ambition, that I want to travel, and that I deserve a woman of your caliber and spirit. I grew up suffering from depression and anxiety. I use to think that everything that went bad was because I wasn't deserving of it but, I know that upon meeting you, that will not be an issue.

Sometimes, it still feels as if I'm still paying for the mistakes that I've made in my past. I'm a work in progress but, I know that I'm not my past. I'm a seed and the enemy will do anything and everything in order to stop me from receiving my blessings and from becoming fruitful. You are a blessing and I want to say thank you. I want to apologize because I know that in order for me to open up, it is going to be painful. I have closed my heart to the world for so long that allowing for someone to touch it… is my greatest fear. However, I am beginning to open up to myself and connect with my higher self in the process. But, I know that if you are the Queen that has been ordained for me, it will be worth it. I'm a man of faith and my word. That will never change. I finally overstand what it means to be a man, King, and uphold the Nazarite Vow. It's a never ending journey of evolving and learning.

I'm not looking for validation, only a chance. I want to do this right. Restoration that only The Most High can create and form. I'm tired of getting this wrong. I want to get it right with you. I want to know your hopes, dreams, visions, gifts, fears, strengths, and more. I know that whatever you are going through, I will not be able to fathom your emotions. I realize that stability can only be obtained by facing our insecurities.

I know that you need your space occasionally in order to recharge and collect. I realize that you're independent. I want to be there when you're going through whatever it is that attacks you. God has a plan for you and you're tapping into it. You're a powerful seed. You're wise, prophetic, strong, and more. The enemy will do whatever it can to stop a child of The Most High from fulfilling their destiny and reaching their purpose. I know that you've been hurt. I know that you've experienced pain beyond my own understanding. I'm in constant amazement of your spirit because the thought of you pushes me to do better. The world, young girls, and women need you. You're tapping into something that no person or enemy can take away.

I want to discover you, comfort you, protect you, cover you, support you, and learn about you everyday in whatever way. I know being single has helped me love myself and become comfortable in my skin. It's a blessing. I don't care about the past, I only want to be a part of your present. I want to pray with you, meditate with you, try new things with you, and be intimate with only you. I feel as if I have been called by God to support you. Whoever and wherever you may be. Words may always sound the same but, rest assure that my actions will never fail. I needed this space and time in order to become stronger for myself and stable enough to support the foundation that has been laid before me.

We are both two books with many volumes. We have been written by the same Author (God) and published by the best company (Spirit). I want to show you the whole and better version of me. Shedding the old is imperative and I'm happy and ready to move forward, leaving the broken pieces. I want God to be in the middle, center, head, and foundation of whatever we do. I have been given a mission in life and I anticipate resistance as a servant to my purpose. It's a blessing. I don't believe in instant gratification. I'm prepared for change and I'm stepping out of what I thought I knew, for God has called me to do something different. There's a separation of the old. After spending more time with God, I realize that service with a mission creates separation of the old. Bringing in the new. What does that mean? It means that I can no longer continue being in this world, the way that I'm comfortable being in. I have to walk into the unknown and submit to the vision. God giveth and God taketh away.

At the same time I find myself moving while wondering. I never realized that my blessings would come from this. I know that a person is meant to be connected to me, when their heart aligns for service in correlation of mine. I don't want the old. I want a new. I have something to offer. I will never be a religious man but, I know that my mission must be The Most High's mandate. Seeking the kingdom. Whatever is not of the kingdom will be shaken and fixed.

I pray that your shoulders become relaxed and your mind becomes at ease but, more importantly I pray that The Most High keeps you safe, surrounded by his heavenly spirits, your ancestors, and gives your spirit freedom. I pray that pain and doubt subsides and brings forth healthy curiosity and love for what God has in store. I just want to see you free. I'm learning that God often times doesn't bring us something new and cast it into the light immediately.

Sometimes, that blessing is put in the dark and then casted into the light in order to increase its magnitude and make it stronger than it would have been, if it were to have started in the light. Jah (God) doesn't want the pretend version of us, only the reality of who we are. It took me a while to realize that. Often times, we are placed in the dark places in order for that magic to occur. I pray that the dead weight stays dead and that God births a new creation. I pray that we stay connected to God and faith grows stronger. I pray for your family and mine. I pray that generational curses/ habits stop here. I pray that the next step taken is a Godly step and that no action shall be taken unless prayed on and ordained by God. I once heard that in order for a man to meet his Eve, he must be an Adam. But, I've come to realize that a man is never an Adam until his Eve has presented herself.

Blessed love Queen,

Nathaniel J. Ali

One of the worst feelings that a changed man can feel is how his old self and insecurities pushed away a woman that he started to fall for. A man will constantly beat himself up because he never had the chance to tell her certain things such as, I don't want to date you for the sake of dating you. I want to date you with intentions. I want to date you, making steps towards the future, while enjoying the present. I see life in you. I see a wife in you. I want to take it slow. I don't just want a few nights with you. I want to fight with you. I'm done fighting with you. You've had my heart since we first met. I see life with you.

That man will regret not being able to tell her the corny truthful things such as, to whom much is given, much is required. I have learned that God gives his toughest battles to his strongest soldiers. My brothers, 9 times out of 10 the woman is going to be stronger than you and you should feel honored to have met God's most prized possession. Ladies, you are the Coretta that every King needs. You are the dream that every man sees. You are the future. The past no longer exists with you. You are a gift.

We can't take the past back nor can we dwell in it but, we can learn from it. I encourage you to do the same. God showed me a vision of this woman and I together, he showed me a glimpse of her and I impacting the world, being happy, being fruitful. But, I can't force it. I can't make a woman see the vision that God has placed within me. More importantly, as I have developed, my reach has expanded so I cannot expect for someone to understand my relationship with God as a King in my own right.

We only need to make sure that we don't repeat the same mistakes again. I'm open to this woman coming into my life because I will be able to love the God in her but, only because I am now able to love and see the God within myself.

I have spent majority of my life hating myself, looking in the mirror with disgust. I have been in pain. I have had nights to where I have cried out of confusion and loss because almost everyone that I have encountered has shown me that I wasn't good enough, in their hearts and minds. But, what I've come to realize is that they were only showing me a reflection of who they were and casting that unto me. I love who I am and who I am becoming. I find it amusing that I am as powerful as I am and I am only 25 years of age... and life is about constantly evolving and becoming better? Two words. WATCH OUT!

Watch out for the man that never had a real childhood. Watch out for the man who has never held hands with a woman in public. Watch out for the man who has never kissed a woman in public. Watch out for the man who acknowledges the boy inside of himself. Watch out for the man who use to be militant to protect himself but, has now become loving and truly knows what duality means.

Watch out for the man that has been constantly rejected and tested by everyone. Watch out for the man who survived after everyone counted him out and walked away. Watch out for the man who has chosen to live. Watch out for the King.

CHAPTER 6
WORDS OF ADVICE

For any man or woman reading this book, please realize that we will never experience true happiness until we partake in true introspection. We must embark on our own quest for freedom and fulfillment. We must look within ourselves and not our partner or worldly things. We must become what we need and stop expecting for someone else to come into our life and give it to us. I stand behind everything that I have stated in this book. I realize that no man or King is truly a King without a Queen to rule by his side. I do not believe in the saying that "behind every man is a good woman." I've developed my own saying, which is that *"beside every King is a Queen and in front of them is God. The only thing that should be behind a man is his woman's hand on his back pushing him forward if he is falling short of his duties."* Queens do not make the mistake of always pushing a man.

If a man cannot push himself then he needs to do some more growing. I will say that there does come a time in every man's life to where life begins to take a toll on him and he will need your support or guidance as a woman because the enemy is trying to pull him down and will be throwing everything at him. I've recently started telling myself to walk amongst men as a silent King but, quiet and humble and a servant to no one but, source. At your service. My brothers, we cannot truly love a woman if we are emotionally disconnected or damaged. Truthfully, we will never be completely healed but, through guidance, prayer, meditation, introspection, increased awareness, and carefulness we can learn to heal our own hearts. We can learn to better manage what it is that we are going through.

My sisters, a man who has never been taught how to properly love or doesn't know what love feels or looks like, should never be walked away from. That within itself is selfish beyond measure for someone to walk away from someone at their lowest point, unless commanded to do so by God in order to help that man grow. If a man has the making of being a King, he will not stay down or at his lowest point for too long and ironically will probably fix himself right after you walk away. Why? *It is not your leaving that fixed him, it was the pain that propelled him forward into his purpose.* There was a switch that went off inside of his head, the act of submission and God directing his footsteps. *A King is slow to act by any measure, even in pain but, once he does act, the world will feel his hand.*

My advice to any woman dealing with a broken man is to understand that it is ABSOLUTELY your right to walk away but, understand that it is selfish. It is justified, unless you walk away and go straight to another man. Then your action is not justified, it is therefore deliberate and somewhat narcissistic. You have every right to put yourself first however, never expect for a man to love you and support you fully at your lowest point if you do not have it in you to do the same for him.

If you cannot be there for a man who is at his lowest point and then decide to leave him, in order to free yourself for someone else. Do not expect for the next man to be a blessing when you did not learn your lesson. The 80/20 rule.

That man that you gave up on, that man that started acting irrational, started questioning everything, and seemed to be quite different because of hardship or trauma is honestly the same KING that you are going to need when you hit your lowest point in life. Why? Because you can acknowledge that you were happy before he started going through what he was going through. If he did not harm you emotionally, mentally, physically, or spiritually then your reason for walking away is not justified.

The good news is that if you choose to walk away from a man who is in pain and you leave him in turmoil, please believe that there is a woman coming behind you who will fight through the storm with him and receive the blessing(s) that this man is about to experience.

Ladies, if you want a man that can be there for you and support you, level you up. Be the same thing for him.

Regardless, if you see that he's dealing with some issues. If he's a good man then talk to him, don't run away. Do not walk away from him or prepare to walk away from him, knowing that he is "dwindling." *Without talking to him, you are helping him to push you away. The end result will be him blaming himself for the whole situation.* If he's a good man then tell him how you feel carefully and explain to him what's going on. Your outlook and perspective on the situation are far more impactful than his because you see it firsthand and from a different point of view. Do not spend your time texting about the problems, that only makes it worse, the man has to try and interpret your tone through text and sometimes the man realizes that you're trying to avoid him and will pick up on that. This only makes the situation worse.

If a man offers to meet up with you over lunch or dinner, take him up on that offer. When you deny him, you are denying him the closure that he is asking for and telling him to seek it elsewhere when that is not the closure that will help him grow the way that he needs to. However, ladies this is NOT your problem. If you deny him closure, yes it is selfish but you cannot help someone grow if you do not want to. Please do not stay in his life if you do not have any intention of helping grow. **MEN YOU MUST FIND CLOSURE ON YOUR OWN.** *It is not the woman's responsibility to give you closure and honestly, it is detrimental to your well being to seek closure from someone that has caused you pain or added to your pain.* **Remember that.**

Men like to talk about their feelings, not text. We function better with face to face interaction better than a phone call or a text message. As a man, we know the type of help that we need. Once we start to become aware of our feelings, we will begin to take the necessary steps to heal that wound correctly and if you deprive us of that, it's like slapping him in the face. You turning down a man that you are dealing with when he is at his lowest point is basically a parody of the movie *300*, displaying the famous spartan kick.

(Man falls down the hole)

Man: Why?

Woman: Figure it out yourself!

Man: But, I already know what's wrong.

Woman: I don't care, figure it out yourself!

Man: I just need to talk to you about it...

Woman: Figure it out yourself!

Man: I'm sorry...

Woman: *(Walks away)*

This is normally the situation and that is normally what is going through the minds of many men who are trying to understand their new found emotions. If a man that you are dealing with approaches you and says that he wants to talk, if he's genuinely a good man then take his word and listen. He will not come to you venting but, he will address the problem and situation. In addition to proposing a solution. That is all that the man wants to do and many relationships are ruined because one person did not want to listen, be supportive, or patient. No relationship starts out perfect and the Romeo and Juliet fairytale does not exist. The end result does. Everyone deserves a happy ending and everyone deserves a second chance. Successful relationships aren't built from the good times, they are built from enduring the struggles while still choosing to embrace the good times.

Godly relationships are built from the times and moments that seemed impossible to get through. They are built from the times that a man has only but one leg to stand on. They are built from the times when a man is lost. They are built from the times when a man or woman decides to be selfish and unselfish at the same time. They are built from hardship and failure. More importantly, they are built from forgiveness and faith. You must forgive that person and yourself.

If you have met someone that is worth the trouble, if you have met someone that has given you more **GOOD** in your life than indifferent, then reconsider. Think about the relationship and all of the possibilities that can come from it. A person could have given you more good than bad but, sometimes a person will walk away because the bad stands out more than the good.

Can I ask you something? Does the good outweigh the bad? I want you to honestly think about this. Does the good outweigh the bad?

If I were to tell you to make a list right now, listing all of the good that this person has done for you, will do it? Of course you will, you've gotten this far in the book, why stop here. So, let's begin. On one side of this paper I want you to list all of the good that a person has done for you and all of the bad that they have done to you. I want you to pray about this, meditate on it, do some true introspection. Turn off the TV, put your phone down and focus. Your life can potentially change for the better:

THE GOOD

THE BAD

_____

_____

_____

_____

_____

_____

_____

_____

_____

_____

_____

_____

_____

_____

_____

_____

_____

_____

_____

_____

_____

_____

_____

_____

_____

_____

_____

_____

_____

_____

After making your list, I want you to think about the relationship and pray on it. Ask THE MOST HIGH for guidance and direction. Balance head and heart when making this decision. If you and a person became physical too soon, then think about it and ask yourself a few questions.

Did they bring joy into my life?

Did they try to support me?

Did they try to be there for me?

Did they give me love?

Did they treat me like the Queen or King that I am?

Did they try?

Did they bring more positivity into my life?

Did I contribute the problems between us?

Think about the quality of the person. Just because you experienced one bad situation with someone does not mean that you two are not meant to be together. One bad situation can last for a month or more if not properly handled. More than likely, you experienced something with that person and it reminded you of something that you have seen or experienced and you pushed them away. You abandoned the relationship and that person. Accept it, you're human.

Note: Also, accept the fact that most people do not abandon someone that they love. They abandon someone that they were using.

This is not me telling everyone to go back to their ex. **I AM NOT SAYING THAT.** What I am saying is that everyone deserves a second chance and just because you became turned off and shut down due to someone's struggle, which led to a behavior, does not mean that they do not deserve a chance. You must consider this, "What if that person doesn't take me back?" If they love you, if they said before that they would wait on you, if they said before that they didn't want anyone else or anything of that nature then the chances are that you have a chance. Consider the timing of everything. How long has it been?

However, if things weren't as clear cut. If you left that person in pain. If you pushed that person away and made them feel as if they weren't good enough, if you said hurtful things to that person, such as "You're not the one for me." I suggest you pray on it and take action. Either leave the situation alone or let divine timing take precedence over the situation. Do NOT create divine timing. **Faith without works is dead and preparation is imperative.** There are probably some women saying right now, "I'm a woman, I'm not chasing man." That's fine, I understand that but, let me ask you something...did that man once chase you? Did you push him away? If the answer is yes then come on Flojo. Get ready.

If that man once pursued you and if it was especially longer than six months or a year and you pushed him away, love it is your turn to come to him. If he loves you and is a man of his word, he will welcome you back. Unless you brought him more pain that positive. There will be hesitation but, he won't be closed to the idea of being with you. He'll be guarded. He'll be reserved. He'll be slow to act in certain situations but, rest assure that when he does you will feel his power. His new found power. This can also be applied the other way my brothers. Listen and read carefully.

Often times, we allow pride and selfishness to keep us from our blessing and we do not take into consideration that God requires us to come to terms with the reality of who we are. We have to get out of the mindset of saying, *"I'm waiting on God"* or *"I'm waiting for God to send me the one."* That's ridiculous. **GOD IS WAITING ON YOU!** This whole time you may have been saying to yourself, I'm waiting on God to send me the one or show me who is for me. Sadly, *he has.* **You just weren't ready to receive it.** Accept that truth. *Some of you passed up God's best for you, for someone that doesn't want the best for you* or for someone who only wants the rest of you, not all of you.

He put this man in front of you and literally said *"Work it."* He put this man, that was probably not the fullest version of himself, in front of you and said *"Work on it."* But, because of this European society and Babylon mindset you may have turned him away because he was lacking emotionally, he wasn't fully self made. Society has told you that it is okay to live your "best life" and not your destined life. *Society has told you that it is okay to be with multiple people, rather than one. That it is okay to be heartless and not hopeful or helpful.*

God will never hand you a whole meal and say "Hear my child, enjoy!" No! He will give you something with all of the ingredients and say, *"Work on it, I have given you this person who possesses all of the ingredients to be the meal that your spirit so rightfully needs. The only catch is that, they need to be seasoned. As God, I alone can only give the proper seasoning but, I need you to take care of this thing or being that has all of these great ingredients. Do not damage them, do not push them away. They may be flawed in certain ways and in regards to certain things that they do, you may not be familiar with but, be still my child. "Why?" Do not question me, I am God! But, if you must know, I have prepared a feast for you and this person and through your labor, every generation after you will enjoy the fruits of your labor."*

THE MOST HIGH put this is my spirit one day and then it became multiple nights. I realize that the woman

**who is ordained for me will have to adapt to that same
mindset.**

Psalm 127:1-2

*"Unless the Lord builds the house, the builders labor in
vain. Unless the LORD watches over the city, the guards
stand watch in vain. In vain you rise early and stay up late,
toiling for food to eat-for he grants sleep to those he
loves."*

I know that it's hard. I know that it is a difficult task
to love a broken man or woman and you may have to do it
from afar but, don't cut them out of your life. If this is a
Godly relationship, meaning ordained by The Most High
then no matter what happened, it will work and be fruitful.

Proverbs 3:5-6

"Trust in the Lord with all thine heart; and lean not unto thine own understanding. In all thy ways acknowledge him, and he shall direct thy paths.

Jah wants to give you a new heart and a *NEW* relationship. I want you to consider that it may be with the man or woman that you pushed away because, they were emotionally damaged. No person will come into our life 100% whole, we and God fill that space. Allow for God to give you a new heart and thus, a new relationship. Don't question and wonder if the other person has changed. Don't question and wonder if the other person will take you back. Pray on it. Pray for it. Take careful and smart action. Balance head and heart and move towards that person accordingly. If they are not willing to open their heart to you, then respect that and understand that this is just one lost battle and we must move forward.

But, if there is hope and God shows you that there is hope, then pray on it. If that person says that they need space and time to gather themselves and adjust in order to welcome you back into their life, then give them that and check in with them periodically to see how they're doing. Why? Because you left. So, at this moment you have to prove to them that they can trust you. Theyy must show you that they have changed and that you can trust them.

Dear Reader,

I pray that you become and have become a better version of yourself. I pray that you walk into who God has called you to be. I pray that any woman reading this becomes a man's Proverbs 18:22. I pray that you become a man's good thing and blessing, giving him favor in the Lord. I pray that you become his Proverbs 31 Queen. Become a wife of noble character, become worth far more than rubies and diamonds, bring good to him and not harm. Become the woman that he can have confidence in. Become a woman who sets about her work vigorously. I pray that any man reading this becomes a woman's Godly husband. Become a man who is not deceived by empty words. Do not be immoral.

Do not be disobedient to God. Realize that you were once in darkness but, are now light in the Lord. Become a man who lives as a child in the light. Become a righteous man. Seek to please the Lord. Forgive yourself for any impurity and for your mistakes. Do not become your mistakes and do not become your past. Forgive yourself from your past. Be very careful with how you live, live wise and not unwise. Understand the Lord's will. Do not get drunk on wine, always be aware. Be filled with the spirit. Always give thanks to The Most High, the Father of Immanuel.

I pray that both of you in return will submit to each other under The Most High's mandate. I pray that your partnership will forever be fruitful and that the blessings from your labor will not be cursed by infidelity or idolatry. Cling to each other, while understanding that space and spiritual isolation is important. Introspection is imperative. Prayer and meditation is a must. Love above everything should be taken in as a daily vitamin and may your kiss to one another become water pleasing to the body.

Shalom,

Signed a formerly broken man who has been repaired and found love in The Most High.

Nathaniel J. Ali

CHAPTER 7
NOTES

This last chapter in the book was not planned. I honestly, ended this book at Chapter 6 but, for some reason something kept telling me to add one more chapter.

Needless to say, here it is, Chapter 7. The biblical number

for completion. I entitled this chapter, "Notes" because this book is a small composition of a few things that I have learned and a part of my perspective that I choose to share with the world in the area of love, relationships, dealing with brokenness, and growing as a man. More importantly as a spirit. Throughout my twenty-five years of living on this earth, I can honestly say that life is about becoming a student in everything that you do and using your gift to teach others. I have dedicated my life to perfecting my craft, gift, and purpose. I realize that your destiny is not your final destination, Zion is. Inner peace.

The Most High, God, Jah, Allah, the Universe, the Divine... whomever you deem as your creator, will not send someone into your life and allow you to become prisoner to your own heart. Two people become connected because of a shared connection however, sometimes those two individuals will not stay together because one will begin to ascend higher than the other. One person will begin to transition into a higher version of themselves, while the other chooses to stay stuck in their ways of living, doing things, and stagnation. Jah (God), will bring someone into your life because you deserve to be loved, you deserve love, you deserve happiness, you deserve compassion and a companion. However, as I stated before. If Jah sees that you two are not equally yoked, or kindred spirits, then you two will be separated quicker than the time it took for you to unite.

Love is a beautiful thing but, self love is where it begins. The ability to love yourself, grow within yourself, do introspection, be content with spiritual isolation, and learning to not conform to the ideas and norms of this world is imperative. I believe that the love that is for me, is for me. No question. When I come in contact with it, I will know it. However, as a man but, more importantly as a spirit, I will not wait on anyone. I will live my life for The Most High, I will continue to learn, evolve, grow, love myself, love my family, and serve God. *Anything you need Lord, I'm at your service!*

If The Most High wants me to build a ministry that is not tainted by the structure of religion, I will do it. If I am told to stand on stage and speak life into people, then I will do it. If I am told to give to the homeless, then I will do it. If I am told to survive and overcome every obstacle put in my path, I will do it. If I am told to be still, then I will do it. *Anything you need Lord, I'm at your service!* When dealing with my spirit, I have no President, I have no Chief-in-Command, I have no leader of a country. My Commander and Chief is The Most High, my Leader is God, my country is nature. My religion is love. The land is my church, not a building. The spirits who are living to grow with a purpose, are my congregation. One love embodies one heart. I do not believe in the military forces because, war is a man made concept. We would not need military forces or weapons, if conquering and destruction was not a thing sought after in the eyes and minds of men. I do respect those select few who have served and risked their life for many. I thank you. To those who have died for many, I salute you.

I do not wish to overthrow a country or prove who is more powerful. We are all meant to live in harmony but, as a soldier of THE MOST HIGH I do believe that certain Pan-African ideals are essential.. I pray that if you are reading this, you become a better person and spirit. Dive into the ocean of knowledge and bask in the rays of love. You are more than what is in front of you. You are more than what you have been through. The meek shall inherit the earth and those who have been overlooked, shall thrive for all eternity. May my words be wine for the body and water for the mind, for either one is pleasure for a limited amount of time. You are the love that you seek. Look within and realize that you have always held the keys to your own heart.

I pray that Jah grants you traveling mercy and grace, abundance, tranquility, peace, love, happiness, protection, and favor. Your work on this earth is not done yet. If you are thinking of giving up, don't. Stop saying that you are waiting on God, that is foolish. God does not work on man's time. God is waiting on you. Time is an illusion, unlimited, and infinite. We are the only thing that is limited but, only by our way of being. Do not miss your appointment. There is more work for you to do on this earth and their is a divine seat with your name on it, that can only be reached by the promise for your purpose.

Blessed love,

A man who has found peace and love within himself.
A Chief. A King.

Nathaniel J. Ali

BETWEEN

By:

Nathaniel J. Ali

I am stuck between inferior and superior

I am stuck between inferior and superior

To the point that it hurts my interior

But you will never see it because of my exterior

Which to you, seems superior

But at times to me, it's like being blind you see

Because I can't help but to feel inferior

My heart has been polluted

There is so much confusion

However, I can still see the horizon

Ignoring all the spies and adding spices to my new recipe

Which goes along with this new melody

So strong and dangerous that they should charge me with a felony

All jokes aside

I'll keep the misdemeanor

Charged in 2015

I'll be cleared by 2018

Never convicted however, the system treats me like a convict

Can barely move my feet

It's like having shackles on my ankles and swimming in a tar pit

It's hard here

You try being a black man

It's like someone put bars here

They look at me like a caged animal

Only this one wears scars and gear

I know the little kid inside me is asking

Who put these bars in here?

I am sorry this happened

Why couldn't I be Aladdin

Be destined to find me a Jasmine

And ride around on a magic carpet

Instead I have shackles on my ankles and I'm swimming in a tar pit

Sometimes the kid inside of me wants to stand up and have fun

But, I have to say

Nah, sit

Watch and observe

Playtime is over

You now have to be a soldier

An upstanding citizen

Realizing that when it comes to the black man

Whites just want to get rid of him

Because of the history and his story

They don't want him to reach his former glory

They show movies and pictures of Egyptians as white

Of Jesus as white

But can't accept the fact that a black man died to save their life

How will you act during the rapture?

Stuck in between

There is only what is and what seems

But, I too had a dream and what seems is far from the truth

The US is suppose to be a land of opportunities

But fails as a community

Some are lost and don't know what to do

The country of red, white, and blue

Is full hatred, jealousy, and what they're teaching is not the truth

I pray for my generation and those that follow

Because if walls are built and hatred grows, there will not be a tomorrow

Riots and protest

We have learned to be peaceful and must continue

But, pardon is such sweet sorrow

Greeks came to Egypt to learn

British and Americans came to Africa to watch it burn

Mussolini tried his best to destroy Ethiopia

But still we stand

I have to profess that we are the better man

I do not hate America

I despise the lies

The fact that the government chooses to ignore the pain in our eyes

When will they learn that they can't burn what clearly walks in the flames

I believe that a time will come when we must leave Babylon

Return to our roots

You cannot hide from the truth

This Babylonian dwelling

Is not selling something that I need to buy

So, why try to deny

Just prepare to make that trip for when the world takes it spin

For then men and women will have to answer to Him

About the Author

"CEO of Tri Fit USA and NALI Nonprofit Corporation, Nathaniel J. Ali has dedicated his life to

 motivating and serving all of mankind. Known for being a Life & Spiritual Coach, as well as a Tedx Speaker he believes that finding your vision and purpose in life is imperative to the ascension and growth of an individual, holistically. As a millennial, he has developed a series of books in order to aid others in their journey of self-discovery.

"I found true love within me, that led to my awakening." - Nathaniel J. Ali

If you would like to know more, please visit his website at *trifitusa.com* "

www.ingramcontent.com/pod-product-compliance
Lightning Source LLC
Chambersburg PA
CBHW050803250626
47155CB00005B/2187